To Mutti
—S.M.

Text copyright ©1997 by Scholastic Inc.
Illustrations copyright ©1997 by Hans Wilhelm, Inc.
All rights reserved. Published by Scholastic Inc.
CARTWHEEL BOOKS and the CARTWHEEL BOOKS logo
are registered trademarks of Scholastic Inc.

Library of Congress Cataloging-in-Publication Data
Metzger, Steve.
    Dinofours: it's class trip day! / by Steve Metzger; illustrated by Hans Wilhelm.
        p.   cm.—(Dinofours)
    Summary: Tara does not want to go on the class field trip to Dino Pond, but when she saves a nest of baby birds she decides that field trips are not so bad after all.
        ISBN 0-590-68993-2
        [1. School field trips—Fiction. 2. Nursery schools—Fiction. 3. Schools—Fiction. 4. Dinosaurs—Fiction.]
        I. Wilhelm, Hans, 1945- ill. II. Title. III. Series: Metzger, Steve. Dinofours.
PZ7.M56775Dhf   1997
[E]—dc20   95-53229
                                                                                                                  CIP
                                                                                                                   AC
12 11 10 9 8 7 6 5 4 3   7 8 9/9 0 1 2/0

Printed in the U.S.A.   24
First Scholastic printing, March 1997

DINOFOURS ™
IT'S CLASS TRIP DAY!

by Steve Metzger
Illustrated by Hans Wilhelm

Cartwheel
B·O·O·K·S ®
SCHOLASTIC INC.
New York Toronto London Auckland Sydney

Today was class trip day!
   Mrs. Dee called the children over to the big rug in the
corner of their classroom.
   "Okay," she began. "Please make a circle."

The children quickly looked for places to sit on the rug.

"Brendan, you're too close," Tara said. "You're sitting on my leg."

"There's no room," Brendan said as he pushed Tara away. "You have to move over."

"All right, children," said Mrs. Dee. "Why don't we all move back a little and we'll have a bigger circle?"

The children moved back.

"That's better," said Mrs. Dee. "Now, who knows what we're going to do today?"

All the children raised their hands. Mrs. Dee called on Tracy.

"We're going to walk through the woods to Dino Pond," she said.

"And we're going to see ducks and frogs!" Joshua shouted.

"And the biggest tree in the whole world!" said Danielle in a clear, loud voice.

"Yes, Danielle," said Mrs. Dee. "Some dinosaurs think the old oak tree next to Dino Pond is the biggest tree in the world."

"It is," said Albert softly. "My daddy told me so."

"Mrs. Dee! Mrs. Dee!" Brendan called out. "Will we eat lunch there, too? My mommy made me three peanut butter and jelly sandwiches."

"Yes," Mrs. Dee said, smiling to herself. "We'll eat our lunches after we arrive at Dino Pond."

Then, Mrs. Dee noticed that Tara's head was down.

"Tara, you've been very quiet this morning," said Mrs. Dee. "What do you think we'll see at Dino Pond?"

"I don't care what we see!" said Tara. "I don't want to go!"

"Why not?" asked Mrs. Dee.

"It's too hot. There are too many bugs. And we're not going to have a story time because of this silly trip."

"I might be able to tell a story if we get back early," Mrs. Dee replied. "And, who knows? Perhaps you'll have some fun."

"I won't!" said Tara.

"Well, we'll see," said Mrs. Dee as she glanced at the clock. "Looks like it's time for us to go. Danielle, it's your turn to be the line leader today."

"Great! I'll pick Tracy to be my partner," said Danielle.

Mrs. Dee helped the other children find partners as they lined up at the door. Tara wanted to be with Joshua, but he was already Albert's partner. The only child left was Brendan. And Tara didn't want to be *his* partner. Today's class trip was getting worse, not better.

"Let's remember the safety rules," said Mrs. Dee as she
gathered the lunches in a shopping bag. "You must always
hold hands with your partner. And you must never, *ever,* walk
away from the group."

The children walked past their playground and on to the
path that led to Dino Pond.

"While we're walking," said Mrs. Dee, "I want you to be nature scientists. Use your ears to listen and eyes to see."

"All I see are mosquitoes," said Tara, "and I hate them."

"Does anyone see anything else?" asked Mrs. Dee.

"I see flowers," said Joshua.

"And I see lots of white clouds," said Tracy.

"Wonderful," said Mrs. Dee. "Does anyone hear anything?"

"I hear sticks crunching under my feet," said Danielle.

"And I hear something growling," said Brendan. "I think it's my stomach. Is it time for lunch yet, Mrs. Dee?"

"No, Brendan," answered Mrs. Dee. "We'll have lunch later on. Please try to be patient."

Tara began to sing a song:

I hate this trip.
It's hot and here's a bug.
Let's go back to school—
For stories on the rug.

After walking a while longer, the Dino Pond came into view.
"We're here!" Tracy shouted.

The children cheered. Except for Tara.
"Is it time to eat?" asked Brendan.
"Not yet," replied Mrs. Dee.
The children walked over to the edge of Dino Pond and looked into the water. They happily pointed out frogs and turtles to one another. Except for Tara.

"Now, let's take a look at the top of the old oak tree," said Mrs. Dee.

If everybody is looking up, thought Tara, *I'm going to look down.*

As she did, Tara noticed something moving on the ground.
Walking closer, she heard chirping sounds. It was a bird's nest!
With three baby birds!

The rest of the children were still looking up at the old oak tree.

"It has a hole in it," said Joshua.

"Maybe a squirrel lives inside," said Danielle.

"I can't see the hole in the tree," said Albert. "There's a branch in the way."

"If everyone moves back a few steps," said Mrs. Dee, "we can all see."

The children began moving backward.
"Stop!" yelled Tara in her loudest voice.

Mrs. Dee walked over.

"What's going on?" she asked.

"There's a bird's nest on the ground," Tara said. "With baby birds. I yelled because I didn't want them to get hurt."

"Look at that!" exclaimed Mrs. Dee. "Tara's right. How did you know they were here?"

"I saw something moving on the ground," said Tara. "Then I heard chirping sounds."

"Tara," said Mrs. Dee, "you used your eyes to see and your ears to hear. You're a real nature scientist."

Tara smiled her biggest smile in a long time.

The children gathered around the bird's nest to get a closer look at the baby birds.

"Please, don't get too close," said Mrs. Dee. "We don't want to frighten them."

"The nest probably fell from a branch," said Joshua.

"Yes," said Mrs. Dee. "And because you found the nest, Tara, you get to put it back in the tree. I'll lift you up. Please be careful not to touch the baby birds."

Mrs. Dee helped Tara place the bird's nest on the branch above them.

"Where's the mommy bird?" asked Albert.

"I don't know," said Mrs. Dee. "But I hope she comes back soon. The baby birds are probably hungry."

"Me, too," said Brendan.

"She'll come back," said Tara. "I know she will."

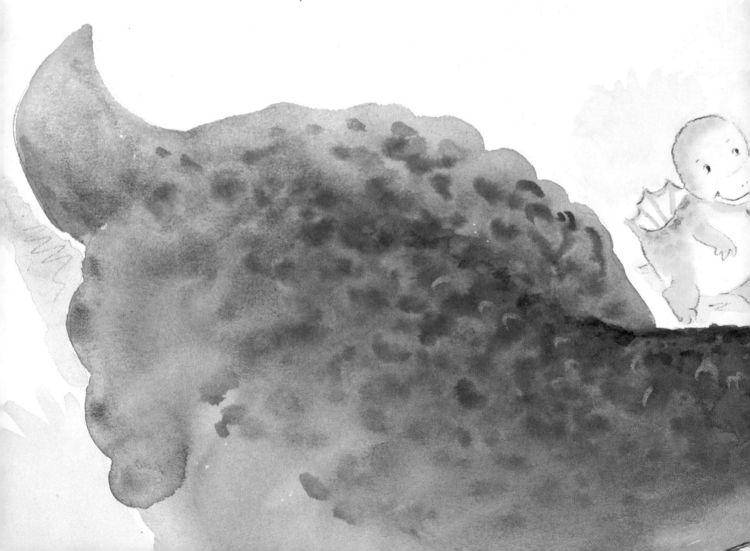

Just then, the mother bird flew back to the bird's nest. After checking on her babies, she flew around Tara's head, chirping loudly.

"I think she's saying 'Thank you' to Tara," Joshua said.

"Yes," said Tara. "She's saying, 'Thank you very much.'"

"Tara," said Mrs. Dee, "when we get back to school, I think we'll have enough time for one new story. Do you have any idea what that story might be?"

"No, I don't, Mrs. Dee," said Tara.

"*How Tara Saved the Baby Birds*," said Mrs. Dee.

The children cheered.

Just then, Brendan walked up to Mrs. Dee.
"Can we eat now?" asked Brendan.
Mrs. Dee looked at the others.
"What do you think?" she asked. "Is it time for lunch?"
They all said "yes" together!

On their way home, Tara sang a happy, new song:

I found the nest,
Sitting on the ground.
Now it's in the tree.
The birds are safe and sound.